Jim Mackey

Laurel Hill

NEW BEGINNINGS

ERIN MACKEY

InspiringVoices®
A Service of **Guideposts**

Inspiring Voices books may be ordered through booksellers or by contacting:

Inspiring Voices
1663 Liberty Drive
Bloomington, IN 47403
www.inspiringvoices.com
1 (866) 697-5313

Because of the dynamic nature of the Internet, any web addresses or links contained
in this book may have changed since publication and may no longer be valid. The views
expressed in this work are solely those of the author and do not necessarily reflect the
views of the publisher, and the publisher hereby disclaims any responsibility for them.

ISBN: 978-1-4624-0778-1 (sc)
ISBN: 978-1-4624-0779-8 (e)

Library of Congress Control Number: 2013918794

Printed in the United States of America.

Inspiring Voices rev. date: 10/25/2013

Table of Contents

Dedication

This book is dedicated to Emily, Kate, Morgan, and Gabe Wilson—my wonderful nieces and nephew. Without you guys, there wouldn't be a Laurel Hill!

Acknowledgments

I want to thank my husband Larry for his love and support that allow me to spend so much time on this passion of mine. I also want to thank my parents, Sue and Jim Cybulski, and my sister and brother-in-law, Jill and Brian Wilson, whose constant encouragement and prayers keep me going. Most importantly, I thank my heavenly Father who gave me this passion and the words for my books. I only pray that each and every book He leads me to write would bring someone to know Him as I know Him.

CHAPTER 1

Birthday Surprises

"Happy birthday, Katie!" Amy yelled as she ran over to her group of friends. Although she was normally shy in public, Amy was bubbly and herself when she was around her best friends. The girls had become friends several years before when they went to a summer camp together as part of a church group. Ever since then, Amy, Jennifer, Morgan, Katie, and Nikki had become almost inseparable. Katie was the youngest in the group having turned ten today, and the rest of the girls were already eleven. Amy was the oldest, as she would be the first to turn twelve in August. Even though Katie was younger, she had been moved up two years in school and was in sixth grade with the rest of the girls because she was so smart. She had always gotten straight A's, and she hardly ever had to study. Sometimes it bothered her older sister, Morgan, because Morgan had to study hard to keep her grades as good as they were. But Morgan was a good student too, so she never got mad or jealous of how easy school seemed for Katie.

"So are you excited about turning ten, Katie?" asked Amy's mom, Mrs. Madison. She worked at Faith Bible Chapel, where the girls and their families went to church.

"I guess so. It's kind of exciting since I'm almost a teenager now," Katie answered.

"Well, enjoy each year as it comes, dear. Believe me, they go by fast enough!" said Mrs. Madison as she walked off to chat with some of the other parents at the party.

"So, Katie, what are you doing tomorrow for your birthday?" Nikki asked.

"Well, after church we're gonna go play miniature golf at Sleepy Hollow. Then we'll go out for pizza since it's my favorite, and dad has some special movie planned at the theater just for us to watch! He won't tell me what it is. He said it's going to be a big surprise," Katie said as she looked questioningly over at her older sister.

"I don't know either, I swear!" Morgan squealed as she threw her hands up defensively.

Just then, Katie's mom announced that it was time to cut the cake, and everyone went over to the picnic table. Mrs. Johnson had spent all day Friday making the food and cake for the party, and everything looked wonderful! The cake was decorated in pink icing with white daisies and green leaves, and it looked good enough that a professional baker could have made it. Mrs. Johnson loved to bake and cook, and since she was a homemaker, she had become very good at baking all sorts of goodies, which always sounded good to Katie and Morgan's younger brother, Gabe. Being four years old, he loved to lick the spoon whenever his mom was done baking.

Everyone sang *Happy Birthday* to Katie, and Gabe made funny faces at his sister as she blew out her candles. Katie blew them all out with one deep breath, and everyone clapped as Mrs. Johnson removed the candles and sliced the cake.

As they ate their cake and ice cream, they chatted and laughed until it was time to open the presents. Katie started opening her gifts but saved the ones from her best friends for last, knowing they would be special.

When she got to them, she opened Jennifer's first. It was a dark blue backpack with her name in white on the front with a little daisy next to it.

"You can keep all of your writing stuff in this backpack, Katie, and use your other one just for school now," Jennifer said. Katie's passion had always been writing stories, and she was quite good at it. All the girls knew she planned to be a writer when she grew up.

"Thank you, Jennifer! I love it," Katie exclaimed with a smile.

"Open mine next, Katie!" Amy shouted excitedly.

As she ripped the wrapping paper off of the small box and opened it, everyone could see the silver pen and pencil set with Katie's name engraved along the sides in black.

"Oh, they're beautiful, Amy. Thank you!" Katie said.

Next Katie reached for Nikki's present. Inside, she found copies of the books *Charlotte's Web*, *Stuart Little*, and *The Trumpet and the Swan*, which she had been wanting for some time.

"You remembered, Nikki! Thank you so much!" she exclaimed as she reached over and hugged her friend.

"You're welcome," Nikki answered with a smile.

Finally, she opened her sister's gift. "I think it's a book," Katie guessed, feeling the present through the paper. As she removed the wrapping, she sat staring at the book. It was a beautiful leather-bound copy of Katie's favorite book, *Anne of Green Gables*, with gold lettering imprinted on the cover and spine.

"It's beautiful," Katie said, still fingering the cover gently as she looked up and saw Morgan smiling at her.

"I know it's your favorite," Morgan said as Katie got up to hug her big sister.

"Thank you so much, Morgan. I love it," Katie whispered as everyone shouted "happy birthday" again.

Mrs. Johnson started to clean up, and Mr. Johnson took Gabe in for a well-deserved nap while the kids went off to play games and listen to music in the backyard. But as they chatted and laughed, every once in a while Morgan would look up to see Katie smiling at her again.

Later that evening, after the party was over and everyone had gone home, Katie went into Morgan's room and asked, "Where did you find that book? I've never seen one like it. It must've cost you way too much!"

But Morgan just answered, "I just happened to find it in a bookstore, and I thought of you," not telling her sister she had saved her allowance for two months to be able to buy the book.

"Thanks, Morgan. I love it, and I'll always treasure it," Katie said.

And as Katie went down the hall to her bedroom, Morgan couldn't help thinking it was worth not buying that new CD she had wanted to see how happy her present had made Katie. And she had to smile to herself.

The next night, the Johnson family enjoyed a very competitive round of miniature golf, which Morgan won. Gabe came in second only because he kept cheating by picking up his ball, walking it over to the hole, and dropping it in. But everyone had a good time.

Then, after enjoying pizza at Ray's, they all settled into one of the theaters at the Movie House, which the Johnson family owned. The last showing of the movie of the week was still playing in the other theater, but the last showing of the movie in this theater had been cancelled so the special presentation for the Johnson family could be shown. As Mr. Johnson settled into his seat and the lights dimmed, Katie waited in anticipation as credits sprang onto the screen and music filled the theater. Everyone began to clap and shout, and Katie squealed as the title flashed up on the big screen: the surprise movie was *Pollyanna*, one of her favorites. Her dad had ordered the movie especially for this night, and it was a wonderful private showing the family all enjoyed.

After the movie, the Johnson family headed home. Katie crept into her bed and thought how this had been the best birthday ever. Nothing could top all the fun and surprises she had had this year. She eventually drifted off to sleep with a smile on her face and a prayer thanking God for how much He had blessed her.

CHAPTER 2

Changes

Maggie Anderson looked nervously at her bedroom clock as she finished tying her shoes and sighed. It was almost time for school, and although normally she loved school, she was hesitant. So much had changed lately with her parents getting divorced and her mom and her moving to Laurel Hill from Connecticut.

Her mom had said they needed to make a change and start over, and Maggie understood why, but that wasn't going to make this first day at her new school any easier.

It wasn't that Maggie was a shy girl, but she just felt a little overwhelmed with everything and not quite ready to try to be Miss Popularity and win over new friends. But she knew it was time to start trying, so she said a quick prayer for courage, lifted her chin, and bounded down the steps and into the kitchen.

"Good morning, Maggie. How are you doing? Are you nervous?" Mrs. Anderson asked.

"Maybe just a little, but I'll be okay, Mom," Maggie answered as she tried to smile.

"Well, I've packed a lunch for you, but I also put a few dollars inside, in case it's not cool to bring a lunch to school," her mom said.

"Thanks, Mom," Maggie replied.

After a quick breakfast and a kiss good-bye, Maggie started out the door to school. Most of the kids walked to school because it was so close to all the residential parts of town. As she walked down the sidewalk, she watched the other kids to see if she could tell who would be in her class. She thought maybe a group of girls walking together up ahead might be her age, but it was tough to tell. Besides, they looked like close friends.

After a couple of blocks, she came to the school. Laurel Hill Elementary School was a large, brick building that recently had a larger gymnasium and library added on to it. In the back, there was a nice play area, a soccer field, and a baseball field. On the right side of the building was the basketball court. Maggie had taken special notice of the baseball field when she and her mom had come to check out the school.

Slowly she climbed the steps and went into the school, heading for the office, just as they had told her to do when she had registered. After talking with the principal for a few minutes, she followed the teacher's aide down the hall and up a flight of steps to her classroom. As the aide stopped and knocked on the door, she heard the teacher call, "Come in," and the door was opened.

"This is your new student, Miss Langley," the aide replied with a smile.

"Thank you, Amanda," the teacher answered in return, and Amanda walked back down to the office. "Well, come in. My name is Miss Langley, and welcome to the sixth grade. Now, what is your name, dear?" asked the teacher. Maggie noticed that she seemed kind, not fake like some adults could be. That was reassuring.

"My name's Maggie Anderson," she said, looking calmer than she felt.

"Well, Maggie, we are very glad to have you. Can you tell us a little bit about yourself? Your hobbies, maybe?" Miss Langley asked sweetly.

Maggie smiled, but she really just wanted to sit down and blend in a little. "I am eleven and a half, and I just moved to Laurel Hill from Connecticut. I like to read a lot . . . I have a pretty big book collection. I also like to play softball and swim, and I love to paint."

"Well, thank you, Maggie. I won't put you on the spot any longer. There's a chair in the back next to Jennifer, so you can take that seat. And again, welcome to Laurel Hill." Miss Langley's words couldn't have come at a better time, because Maggie was beginning to lose her nerve a little. But she walked down the aisle and sat in the open seat.

The girl Miss Langley had called Jennifer smiled, and Maggie smiled back as she set down her backpack. But before either girl could say anything, Miss Langley said, "Okay class, let's get out our math books and begin. Jennifer, could you please share with Maggie until she gets her books?"

"Sure, Miss Langley," Jennifer answered.

Jennifer thought the new girl seemed nice, and when she had mentioned her book collection, Jennifer and Katie had exchanged a smile. She had looked nervous, but who could blame her? It was never fun starting out at a new school, especially near the end of the year. Jennifer decided she would have to find out more about Maggie Anderson . . . but it would have to wait until later.

CHAPTER 3

Lunch Hour

As the class went through one subject after another, Maggie glanced up at the clock and realized it was almost time for lunch. She was still dreading going to the cafeteria, even though the morning had been going okay. Just the thought of sitting alone at a table made her not want to eat lunch. You could always pick out a new kid in the cafeteria sitting by him or herself, with everyone staring and whispering. She knew she was probably exaggerating, but it didn't make her feel any better. Maybe she should just ask this girl Jennifer if she could sit with her. But what if she said no? Maggie didn't think she could take being laughed at on her first day. She decided eating alone for one lunch wouldn't kill her. Maybe she would be able to make a friend before lunch tomorrow and sit with them. She figured worrying about it wasn't going to help, so she said a quick prayer and waited for the lunch bell.

Katie must've been reading her mind, Jennifer thought, as she read the note that had just been quietly passed to her a moment ago.

"Why not have the new girl sit with us at lunch?" Katie had written.

Those very words had just been buzzing through Jennifer's head, and it was nice to know at least one of the other girls had thought Maggie seemed nice. Lunch would be the perfect time to talk with her and get to know her a little better. As the lunch bell rang, and everyone started putting their things away, Jennifer leaned over to Maggie.

"Would you like to eat lunch with us? My friends and I usually bring our lunches, but the regular lunches here aren't too bad, if you have to buy," Jennifer offered.

Maggie couldn't believe it! She had been all ready to brave the cafeteria alone, and now she wouldn't have to. "Thanks, that would be great. I really wasn't looking forward to eating alone. I brought my lunch too," she answered, smiling.

As the other girls came over, Jennifer started introducing everyone.

"Maggie, this is Katie Johnson and her sister, Morgan," Jennifer said as the girls moved toward the door to head to lunch.

"Hi, nice to meet you," said Katie with a smile.

"Hello," Morgan added.

"Nice to meet you both," replied Maggie.

"And these two are Nikki Taylor and Amy Madison," Jennifer added as the group walked down the hall toward the cafeteria.

"Hello," Amy said brightly.

"Hi," Nikki said.

"Hi, nice to meet everyone," Maggie responded.

As the girls walked into the cafeteria and headed for their regular table, Jennifer turned to Maggie and explained, "We usually sit over here."

"How long have you all been friends?" Maggie asked as she took a seat.

"Well, we've known each other for about six years now. We became friends when we went to Camp Wikitoje together with our church group," Morgan answered.

"Wow!" Maggie exclaimed, amazed, "you all go to the same church too?"

"Yeah, we go to Faith Bible Chapel over near Mulligan's Pond," Morgan added. "Does your family go to church?"

"Well, it's just my mom and me, but we went to church back in Connecticut," Maggie answered.

Nikki caught her breath when Maggie had said it was just the two of them, and she had to ask, "Where's your dad?"

"My parents just got divorced about a month ago. Mom decided we needed to move so we could start over," Maggie offered as she lowered her head.

"Oh, I'm sorry," Nikki said. "It's just my dad and me, but my aunt lives with us. My mom died when I was seven."

"I'm sorry to hear that," Maggie said as she looked up at Nikki.

Nikki smiled at her, and Maggie thought there might be a bond between them.

"My mom works over at the church," Amy said. "If your mom is interested in finding out about Faith, just have her ask for Mrs. Madison when she calls."

"Thanks, I'll let her know. I know she wanted to find a new church pretty soon," Maggie said. The girls continued to chat as they finished their lunches. By the time they were back in class, Maggie felt much better. She had made some new friends . . . nice friends. In fact, they had invited her to go with them to the Soda Shoppe after school the next day. As the class began their next lesson, she quietly thanked God for helping her on this first day of school and for showing her such great friends.

CHAPTER 4

Crowler's Soda Shoppe

After school had finished, Maggie walked home with her new friends, talking and laughing and feeling as though she fit right it. She excitedly told her mom all about her first day when she got home, and about the church she could check into for them to try.

Just a block away, Amy told her mom all about meeting Maggie and to expect a call from Mrs. Anderson.

The next day, after school was over, the girls started off toward Crowler's Soda Shoppe. Nikki came up to Maggie and asked, "So, you said yesterday in class that you play softball?"

"Yeah, I started out in Little League, and just a couple of years ago, I switched to softball. My dad was one of the coaches for my old team," explained Maggie. "Is there a team around here for our age?"

"Laurel Hill doesn't have a softball team, but there's a league for the county that I've played with for the past few years. I don't think you've missed the deadline, but you should have your mom call and check into it for the spring season," Nikki offered. "By the way, what position do you normally play?"

Maggie got a little nervous as she answered, "Third base. What position do you play?" She hoped Nikki's response wouldn't be the same.

She could tell Nikki was competitive, and she didn't want to cause trouble so early in getting to know everyone by playing the same position.

"I usually play first base, but I also pitch when we need someone," answered Nikki. "That's great that you play third! We've needed someone for that position for a while."

Maggie smiled, relieved, and agreed she'd have to have her mom call Corbin County's recreational department to find out about the spring season.

As the girls rounded the corner, Maggie noticed the sign for Crowler's Soda Shoppe. Amy had told her at lunch that her dad and Uncle Dan owned and ran the Shoppe. Maggie followed the girls through the door, listening to the bell above jingle, and couldn't believe her eyes. It was just like the old-fashioned soda shoppe from the movies: the counter with the soda fountain and spinning stools, booths and tables, and an old juke box playing fifties music.

"Wow! This place is amazing, Amy!" Maggie exclaimed as they made their way to an open booth.

"Thanks," Amy answered with a smile. "Hi, Dad!" she yelled as she ran up to the counter and leaned over to kiss her father's cheek. "Where's Uncle Dan?"

"Hello, sweetie. He had to go pick up some supplies we needed. How was school today?" Mr. Madison asked.

"It was good. You know, same old stuff. Dad, I want you to come over and meet Maggie," Amy said.

"Sure," Mr. Madison answered as he wiped off his hands and started around the counter. "Hello, girls! How is everyone today?" he asked as he walked up to the booth.

"Hi, Mr. Madison," the girls chorused back. "It was good."

"I know . . . same old stuff, right?" he replied with a chuckle. "So, I guess you must be Maggie. It's nice to meet you." He reached out to shake Maggie's hand.

"Thank you. It's nice to meet you too," Maggie answered.

"How are you enjoying Laurel Hill so far?"

"Oh, it's really nice."

"Well good, I'm glad. Now, ladies, if you'll excuse me, I need to get back to work. Jan will be over in a moment to take your orders. Have a nice afternoon and be safe going home." Mr. Madison turned to walk back to the counter again.

"Thanks, Mr. Madison, we will," answered the girls as Jan walked up with the menus.

After the girls had ordered and were enjoying their ice cream, Katie said, "Maggie, Jennifer and I go to the library on Saturdays for Miss Langley's book club for advanced readers. Would you be interested in coming? I know you said you like to read."

"Sure, that sounds great!" Maggie replied excitedly. "What book are you reading?"

"We're about to start *Lord of the Flies* this week," Jennifer replied. "Have you ever read it?"

"No, but that's one I really wanted to read," Maggie said.

"Great!" Katie added excitedly. "Well, we usually leave at 9:45 in the morning to head over to the library, so we can all walk together, if you want."

"That sounds good," Maggie said. "I'll just check with my mom tonight to make sure it's okay. By the way, we're going to try Faith Bible Chapel this Sunday. Mom said she had actually already called and spoken to Mrs. Madison at the church, and they talked for quite a while."

"Yeah, when I let my mom know to expect a call from your mom, she said she had already talked to her," Amy answered.

As the girls gathered their stuff and headed out, yelling good-bye to Mr. Madison, Maggie bumped right into another girl on the sidewalk outside.

"Oh, I'm really sorry. I didn't mean to run into you," Maggie apologized.

"Well, watch where you're going and you won't have that problem!" the girl quipped nastily.

"Kristi, you know she didn't mean it, so just cut it out," responded Jennifer. "It's not like you're hurt or anything. She apologized, so forget it."

"Just watch it," Kristi snapped, "because who knows what'll happen next time."

"Come on, let's go," said Nikki defiantly. "We don't need to stand around and listen to this."

"No, of course not," Kristi yelled at them as they walked away, "you must have some Bible study to go to or something!"

"*Who* was that?" Maggie asked, still shocked.

"That was just Kristi Lucas," answered Jennifer. "She's in our class, unfortunately, and loves to start trouble."

"Now, Jennifer," Morgan scolded, "you know she has a lot of problems at home, and that her family doesn't go to church. We need to pray for her, not argue with her."

"I know, I know," surrendered Jennifer, "but she really makes it hard sometimes."

"Don't worry about her, Maggie," Katie encouraged. "She's usually not *that* bad."

"Well, that's nice to know," added Maggie, still a little hesitant.

As the girls came to their street, they said good-bye and split off to their houses. As Maggie went up her sidewalk, she was looking forward to the book club on Saturday . . . . but *not* to running into Kristi again!

CHAPTER 5

New Discoveries

When Saturday rolled around, Maggie was relieved. Other than some nasty looks or an occasional comment, Kristi had been fine the rest of the week at school. Why Kristi was like that she just didn't understand. Even at her old school in Mount Royal, Connecticut, she hadn't really dealt with a bully before, just the occasional disagreements between kids that always blew over with time.

But this was different. The girls had told Maggie how Kristi's older brother, Kevin, was in high school and always in trouble. They also said how it never seemed to bother the Lucas family. Kristi's dad had been out of work for eight months now, and her mom had to try to support the family with two jobs. She guessed it sort of made sense how Kristi was acting, but she still hoped everything would just smooth over eventually.

As the girls met along Maple Avenue, Maggie put Kristi out of her mind and focused on the book club. After they walked up the steps of the library and went in, everyone took their seat in the back section of the library as Miss Langley greeted them all.

"Well, hello Maggie! It's nice to have you join us. I'm glad Katie and Jennifer invited you!" she said, and smiled as she handed out copies of the book.

"Thank you, Miss Langley," Maggie answered as she picked up her copy of *Lord of the Flies*.

"As we all know," Miss Langley began, "we are starting a new book today, *Lord of the Flies*, by William Golding . . ."

The time flew by, and Maggie couldn't believe it when the meeting was finished.

"So, what did you think?" Katie asked.

"It was really good! I can't wait to start reading it tonight. But the time went so fast!" exclaimed Maggie.

"I know," agreed Jennifer, "it always does. It never seems long enough."

The girls gathered their things and left the library, discussing the book as they went.

"What do you guys normally do after the book club on Saturdays?" Maggie asked.

"Well, sometimes we get together for lunch or go see a movie," Katie answered.

"Actually," Jennifer added, "we can have lunch at my house and then go swimming afterward, if you guys want. We opened our pool early because it's been so warm out, and my mom already said it was okay."

"You have a pool?" Maggie asked excitedly.

Katie replied, "Jennifer has a *great* pool! It's an in-ground, with a diving board and slide. And they have this really cool old soda machine that you can get sodas from for free!"

"We could call Nikki, Amy, and Morgan to come over too," added Jennifer.

"That sounds great," Maggie answered as the girls came to a stop on the corner of the street. "I just have to check with my mom."

The girls made their plans and went their separate ways. When she arrived home, Maggie burst through the door and excitedly said, "Mom, you won't believe it! Jennifer's mom said we could eat lunch at their house and then go swimming! Their pool sounds amazing! Can I go, Mom . . . *Pleease?"*

"Whoa, slow down!" her mom laughed. "It sounds fine, but first tell me how the book club went."

Maggie filled her mom in on everything as she gathered her things together. And after a quick call to Mrs. Bloom to check on details, Maggie kissed her mom and rushed out the door to head to Jennifer's house.

Down the street, just as Nikki was yelling good-bye to her Aunt Emily and closing the front door behind her, she saw Maggie walking toward her. Nikki hesitated for a second, but then started down her steps to meet Maggie and see if she wanted to walk together to Jennifer's. It wasn't that she didn't *like* Maggie, but for some reason, she just couldn't make herself loosen up around her. They seemed to have a lot in common, especially sports. Maybe she was just jealous. Even though Maggie's dad didn't live with her and her Mom, at least she could still see him if she really wanted to. He was just in a different state.

But Nikki would never have that chance with her mother again. It had been four long years since her mother had passed away, and she missed her so much.

As she waited for Maggie to reach her driveway, Nikki prayed silently, *Lord, please help me to be friendly to Maggie. She's nice, and hasn't done anything wrong, and I don't want to be mean to her. And please help me to not miss Mom so much. In Jesus' Name, Amen.*

And with that quick prayer, Nikki walked over to Maggie with a smile that was a little bigger, and the girls talked as they went on to Jennifer's house.

CHAPTER 6

Lost and Found

The girls were all having fun splashing and laughing in the pool after lunch when Katie asked everyone, "Did you hear Ricky Norman's new bike was stolen?"

"You're kidding!" exclaimed Jennifer. "He just got that bike like a month ago for his birthday! Where was it taken from?"

Katie replied, "He told me he was at Ray's Pizza in town with a bunch of friends after school Friday and when they came out, his bike was the only one missing."

"You know, Karen Rogers' bike was stolen a couple weeks ago too. I wonder if it's the same person, "Amy said.

"Wow!" added Jennifer. "I guess we'd better be careful with *our* bikes from now on. I wonder if anyone else's bikes have gone missing lately."

"I don't know," answered Morgan. "Maybe we should ask around at school on Monday."

"Let's dry off, and we can go watch a movie inside," Jennifer said as she climbed out of the pool.

As the girls grabbed their towels and gathered their clothes together, Maggie suddenly let out a yell.

"Oh no! *Where is it?*" she cried as she began to frantically look under the patio table and along the side of the pool.

"What's wrong, Maggie?" asked Katie as the girls looked questioningly at one another.

"My watch, it's missing! I can't find it anywhere. Do you see it?" Maggie pleaded as she continued to search through the pile of clothes and shoes.

"You're sure you wore it today?" Amy asked as she started to help look.

"I always wear it! I hardly ever take it off. My dad gave it to me before he left. Please, help me. I *have* to find it!" Maggie begged as the other girls started looking for the watch.

"Okay, when do you remember seeing it last?" Jennifer asked.

"I don't know," Maggie cried as she looked around helplessly, tears starting to fall.

"Maggie," Nikki called seriously. "Think hard. What time was it when you last looked at it? Try to retrace your steps from this morning."

After calming down a little and thinking hard, Maggie looked up and said, "I remember I checked the time when the book club was done!"

"I'll go ask my mom if she can drive us over to the library so we can look for it there. I think they close pretty soon," Jennifer said as she started toward the house.

The girls finished picking up their things and walked up to the house with Maggie. "Don't worry, we'll find it," Nikki said reassuringly.

Maggie was still upset, but it helped to have her friends helping. She still couldn't believe how comfortable she felt with them. She had been so worried with the move that she wouldn't make friends quickly, or have anything to do in this new town. But it made her feel better to realize God was really taking care of her. And it was then she realized God was taking care of her watch too, and she knew she would find it with His help. So she calmed down and the girls went into the house.

After the car pulled up to the curb in front of the library, the girls all piled out and bounded up the steps behind Maggie. Katie had suggested that before they started looking all over the library that Maggie ask the librarian, Miss Everett, if the watch had been turned in. So, Maggie hurried up to the desk and looked up at the librarian, only to be met with a very stern look from the woman staring down at her.

"Excuse me," Maggie asked hesitantly, "but has anyone turned in a watch that was found today?"

"You know, it's a shame kids today don't seem to value anything they're given," replied Miss Everett disapprovingly. "Losing things left and right, like they were free. What kind of watch was it?" she added, sounding annoyed as she turned to look under the counter.

Maggie was hurt by what the librarian said. Her watch meant a lot to her, and to hear someone act as if she just threw it aside made her feel awful.

"It's a silver watch with a small heart pendant hanging off the band. It's very special to me. My father gave it to me. I don't know how it could have come off," Maggie answered, hoping the woman would see how important it really was to her.

"Yes, I remember finding it just lying on the floor over near the back tables," Miss Everett responded as she brought the watch up onto the counter. "If it really is that important to you, you should be more careful with it. Things family members give you can mean more than you'll ever know," she said as she handed the watch to Maggie.

Maggie politely thanked Miss Everett, and the girls started to leave, but Maggie glanced back at the librarian and noticed Miss Everett seemed sad as she went back to her work. Maggie wondered if there was some meaning behind the lecture the librarian had given. She would have to ask the other girls about Miss Everett later on.

"Did you find your watch, Maggie?" Mrs. Bloom asked as the girls climbed into the car.

"Yes, they found it. The clasp must be loose. Thanks for driving us over to look, Mrs. Bloom," Maggie answered.

"Not at all, dear," Mrs. Bloom said happily. "Jennifer told me how special it is to you. I'm just glad you were able to find it."

"Yes, I'm glad too," Maggie agreed with a smile as she showed the watch to the group of excited girls.

When they reached Maple Avenue again, Mrs. Bloom let them out so they could walk to their homes, and everyone said good-bye.

As Maggie and Nikki walked down the street together, Maggie glanced over at Nikki. She had noticed Nikki seemed rather quiet in the car, but she didn't want to make her uncomfortable asking about it.

"I'm really glad that you found your watch, Maggie," Nikki said. "I know how much it means to you. My mom gave me this birthstone ring for my seventh birthday. It was the last gift she ever gave me, and I love it more than anything," she added quietly as she showed Maggie the delicate gold ring with the shining opal in the center.

"It's beautiful," Maggie replied in wonder. "You really *do* know how important my watch is to me. Thank you, Nikki, for telling me about your ring. It means a lot to me."

"Sure," Nikki answered with a shy smile. "It's nice to have someone to share it with that understands."

The girls said good-bye, and Maggie headed toward her house as Nikki walked up her front steps. Nikki really *was* thankful to have someone who understood how she felt about her mother's gift. And as she went inside to tell Aunt Emily all about the afternoon, she didn't even realize she was still smiling.

CHAPTER 7

Super Sleuths

When Monday rolled around, the girls were extra busy at school as they asked around about bicycles that had gone missing. And as they walked home together, they compared notes on what they each had learned throughout the day.

"Karen's bike was taken when she was in Video Palace. Her bike was the only one taken, even though there were four or five others parked with it," Amy informed everyone.

"Well, Janet told me her bike was taken right out of her front yard two weeks ago!" Jennifer added.

Katie asked, "But she lives out on Georgia Lane, doesn't she? That's just a block away from town."

"So far, that's five different people who have had their bikes stolen lately, including the two high school kids I heard about," Nikki added as they came to Maple Avenue.

Morgan asked, "How come nobody figured out that so many bikes have been stolen lately?"

"I guess because there's been so much time between each bike going missing. But the really strange part is that they're only taking one bike when there's a bunch of bikes together," Katie added.

"They probably just figured if they try to take more than one bike, it would take too much time and they would get caught," Maggie replied.

"Maybe there's a way we can catch whoever's stealing the bikes," Nikki interrupted. "It *has* to be the same person, and it always happens near town."

Amy looked around at the other girls and asked, "Do you think we really could figure it out?"

"It's worth a try," Jennifer said. "Besides, it's better than just sitting around waiting for one of *our* bikes to disappear. But how could we do it?"

Maggie spoke up, "Maybe we could try to watch some of the places in town where bikes have been stolen and see if anyone looks suspicious."

"Yeah!" agreed Katie. "We could set up across the street or something, so no one would notice us watching them! Maybe we should even use one of our bikes as bait."

"I don't know," Morgan said, a little worried. "Use our *own* bikes as bait? What if we mess up somehow? That's almost making *sure* one of our bikes is taken."

"Well, it's at least worth a shot to watch the bikes that are in town outside some of the stores," Katie suggested.

The girls stood a few more minutes on the sidewalk talking about their first move before they split up and headed home for the day. That night, Jennifer had an idea. She called the girls to fill them in on it, and by night's end, a plan had been set up and the girls were ready to go into action.

Friday finally came. It had seemed like the slowest week ever to Jennifer, but now it was here and it was time to put their plan into action.

As the final bell rang, the girls quickly gathered their things and headed to their lockers. Leaving the school and heading down Bennett Street, they talked excitedly about their next step in trying to catch the bicycle thief. Everyone had thought Jennifer's idea was perfect. They would wait in the town square, hiding in the trees, watching the bikes that would be parked outside Ray's Pizza. On Fridays, there were always a lot of bikes outside Ray's because a lot of the high school kids went there to hang out after school. All they would have to do was watch, and follow whoever they saw take a bike. That way, they could go back and tell Sergeant Mackey where they saw the person hide the bike, instead of trying to stop them themselves. Sergeant Mackey was the policeman who always came to the school whenever there was an assembly about drugs or safety, and the girls had always felt he was a nice guy. He never talked down to the students and he talked to you as if you were an adult, not just a kid.

The girls talked quietly as they got into their hiding place to watch and wait. As the time ticked by and the sun started to go down, they began to think maybe the thief wouldn't come or they had picked the wrong place to watch. Then, all of a sudden, there was some kind of a scuffle in Ray's Pizza. They couldn't tell if it was a fight or an argument, but there was something going on inside.

In fact, the girls' attention had been diverted so much, they almost didn't notice the person pop around the corner from behind Ray's and grab a bike.

"Look!" Nikki whispered. "Somebody just grabbed a bike and snuck around the back of Ray's! Come on!"

The girls raced across the street and behind Ray's, but when they rounded the corner, nobody was there.

Suddenly, they heard some rustling in the woods to their right, and Nikki dashed through the trees with the other girls following close behind. After running a little through the woods, they stopped and listened, but couldn't hear anyone. They had lost the person! They couldn't believe they had been so close! The girls slowly walked back through the woods and across the street to the town square. As they sat down on the park bench, they tried to figure out what had gone wrong.

"Who did it look like, Nikki? Could you tell at all?" Morgan asked.

"No, not really," Nikki answered, looking disappointed. "It all happened so fast. I think it was a boy, but I'm just not sure."

"Well, at least you *saw* something!" piped up Katie. "We almost totally missed the bike even being stolen because of that fight in Ray's!"

"Yeah, what happened in there, anyway?" Morgan asked, a little annoyed.

"I don't know. It looked like a couple of people pushing and yelling," Maggie answered. As the girls all looked across the street toward Ray's again, she added, "It seems to be quiet now."

"Come on, we'd better get home," Nikki said as she looked down at her watch. "Besides, I don't think anything else will happen tonight."

So, the girls all walked away toward Maple Avenue, still talking about what had happened. But as they left, Jennifer glanced back at Ray's one last time, and happened to see Kristi sneak out the front door and look around the corner of the building toward the woods at the back. Then she slowly walked back into Ray's looking very worried.

Now, what was that all about? Jennifer thought, trying to figure out what Kristi was up to.

But just as she went to mention it to the other girls, Maggie had an idea she asked Jennifer about. By the time they all parted ways to go home, Jennifer had forgotten that quick glimpse of Kristi . . . for the time being.

CHAPTER 8

Cops and Robbers

On Monday, as the girls walked to their table in the lunchroom, they talked about the missing bikes again. It had been the main thing they talked about since their failed attempt at being detectives, but they hadn't thought up any new ideas about what to try next.

"I heard it was Jason West's bike that was taken Friday," Morgan said.

"Yeah, he was really mad when he came out of Ray's," Jennifer added.

Just then, Kristi walked by their table and overheard what they were talking about. Nikki looked up, expecting to hear some smart comment, but was surprised to see Kristi turn and walk away from them, looking a bit nervous.

"Well, that's a first!" she declared. "Usually Kristi has a nasty comment about *everything* we say. I wonder what's up with her. She looked almost afraid!"

Suddenly, Jennifer exclaimed, "Oh!"

All the girls looked at Jennifer to see what was wrong, but she was already gathering up her lunch.

"What is it, Jennifer?" Amy asked, looking questioningly at the others.

"Come on, we've got to go," Jennifer replied in a serious tone. "We've got to talk, but not in here. Let's go outside and finish lunch near the Tree."

The girls all quickly gathered their things and followed her out of the lunchroom through the side exit.

The Tree, as it was known, was a big oak on the side of the building where the kids would sometimes go to eat lunch. You could still hear the lunch bell, and as long as there wasn't any horsing around or fighting, the teachers let the students use the area at lunchtime.

They all walked up to the Tree and sat down, taking what was left of their lunches out again.

"Now, what is going on, Jennifer?" Nikki asked finally as the group sat in wonder.

"Just wait a minute," she answered secretively as she looked back toward the exit door they had come through.

Morgan laughed, a little nervous, and said, "You look like someone was spying on us!"

Finally, Jennifer said, "I'm sorry, but I wanted to make sure she didn't follow us out here. I had forgotten all about it until Kristi came up to the table. I saw her come out of Ray's Friday after the bike was stolen!"

"So?" Morgan asked. "She's in there a lot with her brother and his friends."

"No, but this was weird," argued Jennifer. "She came out when we were leaving and peered around the side of the building and went back into the pizzeria after she looked. And then, just now, she acted scared when we were talking about it!" Jennifer paused, and then added, "You don't think she has something to do with the stolen bikes, do you?"

"Jennifer!" scolded Amy. "You shouldn't say something like that, even if you're kidding! You can't just accuse someone of stealing without any proof."

"But wait," Maggie added, "didn't you say she's in there with her brother and his friends a lot? And you said before that her brother Kevin was always getting into trouble."

"Do you think Kevin and his friends are the ones stealing the bikes?" Morgan asked.

Jennifer added, "When I talked to Jason West, I asked him what happened in Ray's. He said Kevin was teasing Kristi and trying to pour his soda on her head, and she was yelling at him and pushing him away. That was the commotion we heard!"

Katie added, "Then, if he was involved, he might've been distracting everyone so someone else could steal the bike. But who?"

"Probably one of his friends," Nikki said. "It could've been any of them, but they're probably all in on it."

"But what about Kristi?" Amy asked hesitantly. "Do you think she's part of it . . . helping them?"

The girls were quiet for a minute, but it was Nikki who answered. "No. She looked too scared. But I think she figured out what Kevin was doing, and she's scared he's going to get in trouble."

"I say we go confront her," Morgan said determinedly.

"No," Amy replied. "If she does know what is going on, we shouldn't be the ones to ask her. I told Uncle Dan about what we did Friday. He said we had to be careful about what we said and did, and that we should just let the police know if we found anything out. We might mess up the investigation, and they wouldn't be able to do anything to whoever was stealing the bikes. He suggested we talk with Sergeant Mackey at school this week."

"Yeah," Nikki agreed. "We still don't have any proof, but if we tell him about Kristi and what we saw, he could talk to her and find out what's going on."

So, the girls cleared up from lunch and went back into the school to finish the day's classes. After school, they all went to Crowler's and told Uncle Dan what they had discussed. He called the Laurel Hill Police Department and asked Sergeant Mackey to come down to Crowler's Soda Shoppe, and when he arrived the girls told him about Friday's escapade and their theory.

"I know we don't have any proof," said Amy quietly, "but we figured you could find out what it all means. We didn't want to mess anything up."

"Well, that's good thinking, young lady," Sergeant Mackey replied. "You girls are very ambitious, and I thank you for wanting to help. But, next time, no chasing criminals, okay? Let's leave that to me!" he added with a wink and a smile.

"Okay," the girls answered together, and Sergeant Mackey left, promising to let them know what he found out.

It was Wednesday at lunch when the girls heard the buzz around the cafeteria that the stolen bicycles had been found and the thieves caught, but no one had heard who it was.

"Wow!" exclaimed Jennifer. "Do you think . . . ?" And they talked about it all through lunch.

That night, Sergeant Mackey came to Mr. and Mrs. Madison's house to tell them what the girls had done, and that they had given the police the "tip that broke the case." Then, he told them it was Kevin Lucas and his friends who had stolen the bikes.

"Now, I want to assure you both that I already gave the girls a thorough lecture, and they have promised not to play Nancy Drew anymore," he told the Madisons.

"Well, thank you, Sergeant Mackey," answered Mrs. Madison, relieved. "I think these girls have had enough excitement for now anyway!"

Sergeant Mackey said goodnight as he went to make his way to a few more homes that evening. After he had gone, Amy had to tell the whole exciting story again to her parents!

CHAPTER 9

The Big Parade

That next week was one excitement after another for the girls. Everyone at school learned how they had tried to catch the thief, and they became celebrities for a little while. The other kids asked about that night at Ray's, and weren't they scared one of their bikes would have been stolen? It was exciting at first, but the girls got tired of answering the same questions over and over, so after a few days they were ready for their fifteen minutes of fame to be over.

Another surprise was finding out that Kristi had helped Sergeant Mackey by turning in her brother Kevin and his friends. Kristi was very quiet at school, and didn't really like to talk about it. Maggie thought she looked sad . . . when she wasn't busy being her mean old bossy self.

It must be really hard to be in a family that doesn't look out for each other, Maggie thought. *I think I'll try and pray extra hard for her.*

Maggie even tried to be friendlier to her, but Kristi just took each opportunity to try to put her down or make fun of her. So, Maggie figured praying would work the best and decided to just keep her distance.

When Friday came, things were finally starting to calm down a little at school as everyone slowly forgot about the stolen bikes. Memorial Day was coming that weekend, and all the kids were looking forward to it. School would be closed on Monday, and Laurel Hill would have its annual Memorial Day Parade. But then, something amazing happened. During morning announcements, the principal said there was going to be a brief assembly after lunch.

"Wow! I wonder what's going on," exclaimed Katie excitedly. "Do you think it's about the parade on Monday?"

"Maybe," answered Amy. "Maybe there's something special going on this year!"

The whole school was buzzing all morning, and the kids didn't do much concentrating in class. Finally, after lunch, all the students were in the auditorium waiting for the big announcement. Up on stage, Principal Curtis walked over to the microphone. And walking up next to him was Mayor Cooper!

What's he doing here? Morgan wondered.

"All right now, kids," began Principal Curtis, "let's settle down. Now, I've called you all together today because Mayor Cooper wanted to speak to you a moment. So, let's make sure we give him our full attention, okay? Mayor . . . ," Mr. Curtis added as he stepped away from the microphone to let Mayor Cooper speak.

"Thank you, Principal Curtis," Mayor Cooper began, "and thank all of you students and teachers for letting me take up a few minutes of your time here today. Now, as everyone knows, Monday is Memorial Day, and we will be having our annual parade."

The children clapped, cheered, and hollered in response.

"Yes, I know, it's always a great holiday . . . and a great way to get a day off from school," Mayor Cooper added with a smile as everyone laughed. "But, we have something extra to celebrate here in Laurel Hill, and that is why I am here today. Thanks to the courage and smarts that were shown by a few young people recently, they were able to help the police stop some thefts. So, we are going to have these young people lead our parade Monday by riding their bikes along the route."

Everyone began talking and whispering, and the girls all looked at one another with shocked expressions.

"Now, the young people I am speaking about are: Jennifer Bloom, Amy Madison, Morgan and Katie Johnson, Nikki Taylor, Maggie Anderson, and Kristi Lucas. So, make sure you congratulate them, and cheer them on Monday. Thank you all for your time, and have a nice Memorial Day, everyone!" Mayor Cooper added.

Principal Curtis dismissed everyone back to their classes, but everyone was talking about the parade on Monday.

All weekend, the girls anxiously prepared for the parade. They washed their bikes and picked out what they would wear in the parade. They were each going to wear something red or blue so they would match. Jennifer even picked out some red, white, and blue streamers to attach to their bikes, so they would wave behind them as they rode.

At the Taylor house Sunday night, Nikki, Mr. Taylor, and Aunt Emily talked about plans for the summer as they ate dinner.

"So, when is camp starting this year, Nikki?" Aunt Emily asked.

"I think it starts June 21, but I don't think our group from church is going until the third or fourth week this year," Nikki answered.

"Well," continued Aunt Emily, "I was thinking that with the end of school coming up so soon, you girls should probably try to plan something nice to do for the end of the school year. How about I take you all to Adventure Park the Saturday after school lets out?"

"*Really?*" squealed Nikki. "That would be awesome! Could we have a sleepover the night before, so we could leave from here?"

"Sure," Aunt Emily answered with a smile. "That sounds like a good idea. Why don't you mention it to the girls tomorrow, and we can get the plans arranged with all of the parents?"

As the girls gathered before the parade, Nikki told them all the big plans.

"What's Adventure Park?" Maggie asked.

"You've never heard of Adventure Park?" Katie replied. "Wow, you're gonna love it!" So, they all filled Maggie in about the park as they waited for the parade to start.

The master of ceremonies blew the whistle at exactly noon, and the color guard began to march down Johnson Drive from the school parking lot. The police department walked behind the girls in their dress uniforms, and Sergeant Mackey gave them all a smile and a wink, as they rode in front of them on their bikes. Next came a few bands from the high school and the junior highs. Then the fire department followed with their Dalmatian sitting in his seat on the fire engine. Then, other groups followed in the parade as well: the majorettes, 4-H, and some city council members riding in antique cars.

The only disappointment of the afternoon was that Kristi had decided not to ride in the parade.

I don't understand it, Amy thought, *she did a lot more than we did to help.*

Other than that, to the girls it seemed like the best Memorial Day Parade in Laurel Hill history!

CHAPTER 10

Last Days

The next two weeks seemed to crawl by as everyone waited anxiously for school to be over. The tests and lessons were basically finished, so students spent their time turning in books, cleaning out their desks and lockers, and helping the teachers clean the rooms up for the end of the year.

The last day of school was on a Thursday, and it was a half day. That Friday was the slumber party at Nikki's house, and the trip to Adventure Park was on Saturday. But the girls had made their own plans for Thursday.

After the last bell had rung, the girls went down the street together and had lunch at Crowler's. Then they changed into their swimsuits, which they had left there ahead of time, and headed down to Mulligan's Pond to swim the afternoon away.

They had chicken fights, played on the tire swing, and practiced their dives and cannonballs off the dock in the middle of the pond. Their fingers were prunes by the time they pulled themselves out and laid on the grassy bank to dry in the sun.

Finally, they got dressed over their swimsuits and walked to the Movie House and watched a movie together. Later, as they said their good-byes and split up to head home, they made sure their plans were all set for the following night at the sleepover.

"Now, they all know to come over at four o'clock for dinner, right, Nikki?" Aunt Emily asked . . . for the third time that day. *She* was as excited about the weekend as the girls were!

"Yes, Aunt Emily," Nikki answered with a laugh. They had talked about their plans for two weeks and had every last detail planned out. "I think Amy's here!" she shouted excitedly.

When all the girls had arrived, Aunt Emily let them know the pizzas would be there soon, but she had snacks in the dining room for anyone who wanted them.

"I have a bunch of CDs we can play," Nikki suggested.

"Ooh, good!" added Morgan, "I got a new CD I haven't listened to yet, so I brought it with me!" So, the girls listened to music, sang to their favorite songs, and danced until the pizza arrived.

"Now, I was under orders to pick out some good movies, so I hope I accomplished my mission," joked Aunt Emily. "Take your pick of what you want to watch, and give a call if you girls need anything."

"Thank you!" they all chorused.

So, the girls settled down in the family room with their pizza and a scary movie. But after about fifteen minutes, they voted to change movies and watch something funny instead.

When the movie was over, Nikki asked, "Do you want to watch another movie, or play some games instead?"

"Let's play some games," Morgan volunteered. "We watch a lot of movies at the Movie House!" They all laughed and went into the guest room to look for a game they could play.

"Wow! *Twister!*" Jennifer shouted excitedly. "Let's play this. *Twister* is always fun to play!"

So, the girls brought a few games out into the family room, and after some convincing, they even talked Aunt Emily into playing with them, and Mr. Taylor was elected the "official spinner."

"Right foot red!" Mr. Taylor announced.

"Jennifer, your knee is pushing my nose off my face!" Amy said, trying to bend her head back out of the way.

"I'm sorry, Amy," Jennifer answered, laughing, "but I'm almost sitting on Katie as it is!"

"I know!" Katie added, as they all began to laugh.

"But now, I have to sneeze!" Amy sniffed. And as she sneezed, everyone laughed, and the pile collapsed into a heap of legs and arms and laughing girls on the floor.

"Okay, how about a non-contact game of *Monopoly?*" Aunt Emily suggested. "We can even make some ice cream sundaes, if you'd like."

"Yay!" they all cheered as they clamored for the kitchen.

After playing for a couple of hours, they had to call the game a draw because it was getting so late and no one was close to winning. Katie and Jennifer kept landing on each other's properties and paying each other rent. Poor Maggie kept paying the Luxury Tax or picking a bad Community Chest card. And Amy was stuck in jail for most of her turns. But they agreed they had a lot of fun playing.

"I have your sleeping bags set up in the family room, girls. Try not to stay up all night," Aunt Emily announced, adding, "We don't want to get too late a start in the morning."

"Okay, good night!" the girls chorused. "Thank you, Aunt Emily! Thank you, Mr. Taylor!"

"Sleep well, girls, and you're always welcome," Mr. Taylor answered as he kissed Nikki goodnight.

Once the girls were settled and the lights turned out, it didn't take very long for everyone to drift off to sleep and dream about all they would do the next day at Adventure Park.

CHAPTER 11

Water Slides

The next morning, Aunt Emily let the girls sleep in until nine o'clock, since they had been up so late the night before.

"Okay, sleepyheads!" she announced. "Time to rise and shine! We don't want to get to Adventure Park *too* late, or the lines will be too long to go on anything." As she helped Maggie roll up her sleeping bag a few minutes later, she added, "There are muffins, fruit, and juice in the kitchen for breakfast, so feel free to help yourselves, girls."

And as the sleepy girls roused themselves, the excitement spread throughout the group as they discussed their plans for the day.

"I really want to go on the Plunge today! They say it goes up twenty-one stories!" exclaimed Nikki.

Jennifer added, "So long as we can go on the Tsunami Slide sometime. I think it's supposed to be pretty warm out."

"What about the safari?" Katie asked. "Do you think we'll have enough time today, Aunt Emily?"

"We'll have to see what we are able to get to, girls," she answered, grinning. She loved that they all called her Aunt Emily, not just her niece Nikki. She looked down at her watch and quickly added, "But if we don't leave now, we may not have time for *any* of it!"

So, with a last-minute dash around the house to be sure nothing was forgotten, the girls all hustled outside and climbed into the van. As they started on their hour-long drive, the girls turned on the radio and sang to their favorite songs.

The van pulled up to the park's entrance at ten-thirty, and the girls were giggling and talking so much it was difficult to understand what any of them were even saying.

"Can you even hear each other? You're all talking at the same time!" laughed Aunt Emily.

After parking the van, the excited group raced to the ticket window. Once inside the park, Aunt Emily asked, "Where do we go first? Have you all set up a plan of attack, or is it still being debated?"

"I think we all agreed we want to go on the Mongoose first, since it's so new. Hopefully, there won't be a line this early," announced Morgan.

Amy added, "Yeah, and we want to wait to go on the Tsunami Slide later, when it gets warmer."

"Okay, the Mongoose it is!" Aunt Emily stated.

So, they all set off to begin their exciting day. They rode the Mongoose twice, it was so much fun. Then, they went on some smaller rides, like the swings and the Ferris wheel.

While they were riding in the bumper cars, the girls decided to chase Aunt Emily's car and try to get her into a corner. But, she turned out to be a rather skilled driver, and the *girls* were the ones who wound up stuck! Jennifer was spinning in circles for a little while, until the attendant could straighten her out. Maggie kept bouncing between two stopped cars and couldn't get her car free. And Nikki wound up being chased into a corner by Aunt Emily, and was bounced around a little. But everyone was laughing and having a wonderful time.

When it came time to go on the Plunge, Amy and Aunt Emily decided to just watch. "I don't like those high drops," admitted Aunt Emily. "I'll stay down here, and maybe Amy will keep me company."

The girls decided to stop for lunch after they had "taken the Plunge," so they went over to the food court in the center of the park. It had every kind of concession stand and every kind of food that could be desired. A couple of the girls got hot dogs and boardwalk French fries. Another one decided on pizza, and still a couple more went for tacos. Everyone was enjoying the food and fun so much they couldn't believe how fast the time was going by.

"So, how late *can* we stay, Aunt Emily?" Katie asked.

"Well," Aunt Emily answered, "I figured we could at least stay until dark, because it's neat to ride the rides when they are all lit up. But we shouldn't stay too late, since we have church tomorrow."

So, the group began to plan out their afternoon very carefully so that they didn't miss one thing they wanted to do. They decided to head on over to the boardwalk games area after lunch.

Nikki won a stuffed bear by sinking two out of three basketballs. Jennifer was trying her luck at the ring toss, but wasn't having a lot of success, and Maggie turned out to be a sharpshooter at the water balloon race, winning a crazy hat.

Then, everybody rushed over to the Illusions Theater to watch the 3-D film. It was actually like *being* there in the movie as you stood and watched. They showed a parachuter falling and then being pulled up by the open chute. Then, it was someone flying down a zip-line, and finally someone high diving into a pool. It almost felt as if they got wet as the camera hit the water.

When it was over, they decided it was time to go on the Tsunami Slide. They all started across the park, but stopped in front of the fountain near the food court when they saw some people having their pictures taken.

"Oh, can we do that, Aunt Emily?" Nikki begged. "We could get those key chains with our pictures in them!"

After a few minutes of pleading and begging, Aunt Emily finally answered, "Okay girls, all right, I give up! You only live once. Let's do it!" So they all rushed over to be next. They decided to do a group picture in front of the fountain, so each girl could get the same picture in her key chain. But, after the camera flashed and Aunt Emily walked over to get her claim ticket for later, they suddenly heard someone say, "Oh, isn't that sweet! It must be Bible Day at the park!"

"Oh, great!" sighed Nikki as the girls turned to see Kristi standing off to the side with a few of her friends. "What do you want?!"

"Nothing from you!" Kristi snapped. "I'm just glad I'm with people who really know how to have a good time. Not a bunch of goody-goodies!"

But before Nikki could respond, Maggie stepped forward and said, "Well, that's great, Kristi. I hope you have a great time! We have to be going now. Come on, girls." She took Nikki by the arm and guided her as they all started to walk away.

Kristi wasn't finished, however, so she followed after them, yelling, "Hey! Where do you think—" But suddenly she was cut off and the girls heard a splash.

They whirled around to see Kristi standing up in the fountain, dripping wet. She had slipped on the wet pavement surrounding the fountain and fallen in. As they all began to laugh, Aunt Emily walked up and said, "Well, we'd better hurry off now, girls," as she tried to keep the laughter to a minimum. The girls followed Aunt Emily as they all walked away, and Kristi was left by herself to slosh out of the fountain and yell at her friends for not helping her.

For the rest of the afternoon, the girls went on all their favorite rides . . . riding some more than once. And as it began to get dark, they all bought glow necklaces and decided to ride on the gondola that went over the whole park so they could see everything. It was a beautiful night, and everything looked magical all lit up.

"Look!" cried Amy. "There's the fountain, and they have all different-colored lights in the water!"

"And there's the carousel!" shouted Katie.

They stopped and picked up their key chains with their pictures just before they walked out to parking lot, and the girls all squinted into the key chains as they held them up toward the lights, trying to see how the pictures looked.

As they drove home from Adventure Park, everyone was much quieter. Morgan quietly asked, "Maggie, why did you stop Nikki from saying anything to Kristi? She was the one who was starting trouble, after all."

"Well, I just figured she could only ruin our day if we let her. Besides, she's been through an awful lot lately with her brother," she answered.

"Well, I think you did a good job, Maggie," Amy replied. "Besides, I think Kristi got what she deserved . . . even better than we could've given!" And they all giggled as they remembered how she had looked soaking wet in the fountain.

But Aunt Emily had a smile on her lips at how Maggie had handled the situation, and the whole drive home she kept thinking how proud she was of these girls.

CHAPTER 12

Family Matters

That following Monday during breakfast, Mrs. Anderson told Maggie, "Now, it's almost your birthday, and you still haven't told me what you would like to do for your party."

Maggie hadn't really thought about what she wanted for her birthday party. The months since they had moved to Laurel Hill had flown by so quickly, she could hardly believe her birthday was almost here. "I don't know, Mom," she answered. "But I'll try to think about it and let you know soon."

"All right, but you need to let me know by tomorrow. I'm not going to have a lot of time to set everything up, you know. As it is, your birthday is less than two weeks away!" Mrs. Anderson replied.

A few minutes later, as Maggie went out the front door and walked down Maple Avenue heading to meet up with the other girls, she thought about the past few months at Laurel Hill. Before they had moved, she had been so sure she was going to hate it here. Her birthday party had been the farthest thing from her mind. *Who wants to have a party without friends?* she had thought, being afraid it would be a while before she made friends at the new school.

But things were certainly different from what she had feared! She had good friends who she couldn't even imagine not spending time with now, and a nice church that was just like their old one in Connecticut. She knew

God had really blessed them, and that she could trust Him to take care of them. "Thank you, Lord," she prayed as she walked down the street. "I knew that You would take care of us, but You have done so much more! Thank You for bringing us to Laurel Hill." And she hurried ahead to Jennifer's house, so she could ask the girls to help her figure out some birthday plans.

"I didn't know it was your birthday already!" Morgan said excitedly. "Do you have any ideas what you want to do?"

"I don't know," Maggie answered, "I really haven't been thinking about it that much. There's been so much going on these past few months."

"Well, let's give her some ideas," Amy spoke up as she turned and looked at the other girls for help.

"Okay," Katie replied, "there's miniature golf, like we did for my birthday. That's always fun."

"Or the skating rink at Canyon Run. It's only a half hour away, if you like roller skating," Nikki volunteered.

"Hey, wait, what about Fun Land?" Morgan added. "It has a little bit of everything!"

"What's that?" Maggie asked. If it was anything like Adventure Park, she knew it would be too expensive for her party. But she wanted to do something the girls thought would be fun.

"Fun Land would be perfect," Nikki answered. "It's only about fifteen minutes from Laurel Hill, and it really *does* have everything! Batting cages, miniature golf, go-karts, and paintball. They even have an arcade and a few water games."

"What do you think, Maggie?" Katie asked as the girls all waited for her response.

Maggie hesitated. "Well, it sounds great, but is it real expensive? I hate to ask, but I know things are tight right now, since the move and all."

Amy responded, "No, it's a small place. It's nothing big like Adventure Park."

Maggie smiled. Sometimes she thought they read each others' minds a little. But she replied, "I think it sounds perfect. Let's go over to my house so you can help me tell Mom about it."

So, Maggie called her mom and checked to make sure it was all right, and the girls told Mrs. Bloom where they were going. When they all got to Maggie's house, they excitedly told Mrs. Anderson about the birthday idea and made plans for the party.

But as they were all talking, Nikki pulled Amy aside. "Amy, I was going to invite Maggie to go to Camp Wikitoje with us next month, but now I don't know what to do! She was so worried about the money for her birthday party, and now this would cost more. What do you think?" she asked dejectedly.

"I think you should still invite her, Nikki," Amy answered. "There are always ways to earn the money for camp, if we have to. Remember when we wanted to build the tree house?"

"That's right," Nikki said excitedly, "we did those bake sales and stuff all summer, and we earned enough for the tree house! That's a great idea, Amy!"

And as the girls walked back into the kitchen, Nikki had a big smile on her face. *I'll wait to mention it to her,* she thought, *just so she doesn't get worried about the money now and ruin her excitement. There's plenty of time.* So they all talked and laughed as they made plans for Maggie's party.

A few days later as the girls hung out in that very same tree house at Amy's house, Nikki looked over at Amy questioningly, and Amy gave Nikki a quick nod.

"Maggie," Nikki began, "I wanted to tell you something."

"Sure, Nikki, what is it?" Maggie answered as she laughed at something Morgan was saying.

"We wanted to ask you to go with us next month to Camp Wikitoje when the church group goes. It would really be great if we all could go together," Nikki said. Everyone grew quiet as they waited for Maggie's answer. But when they looked over at her, she was looking down at the floor sadly. This was what she had been dreading for the past couple of weeks. She had heard all about the camp at church, and had even picked up one of the brochures so she could ask her mom about it. But when Maggie had seen the cost for the week's stay, she knew they couldn't afford it. Not after the move *and* her birthday party. It would be just too much. In fact, she hadn't even asked her mom, because she didn't want her to feel bad that she wouldn't be able to send her.

Bravely, Maggie looked up and replied, "I wish I could go, but I don't think I can this year. It's just too much money, especially after the move, and now my birthday party. But I should be able to go next summer," she added with a smile.

Jennifer asked, "What about asking your dad to pay for it?"

Maggie became a little red as she answered, "No, Mom would feel like we couldn't make it on our own. I couldn't do that. She's been working so hard . . . ." But Maggie had to turn away as she became teary. She knew it had been a hard move for her Mom, even though it was a good move for them.

Amy piped up with a knowing glance at Nikki, "Maggie, don't worry. You'll be able to go to camp this year."

Maggie looked up quickly to protest, but Amy interrupted her. "We can all help you earn the money by next month. We did it a few years ago when I wanted to get this tree house."

"That's right!" added Katie. "We had car washes and did babysitting, and we were able to save up enough!"

As the girls talked about it, trying to convince Maggie, she realized they really wanted her to go with them. "Well," Maggie finally said, "I guess we could at least *try*." And all the girls hugged her and began telling her all about the camp and the great times they would have.

CHAPTER 13

Best Friends

The next week flew by faster than imagined, until one sunny morning, Maggie awoke to her mother singing "Happy Birthday."

"So, do you feel any older?" Mrs. Anderson asked as Maggie yawned and stretched in bed.

"No, not really," she answered sleepily. "I can't believe it's really my birthday! It feels like we just moved here."

"I know," Mrs. Anderson replied, "these few months really have gone by fast. Do you regret moving here, Maggie?"

Maggie looked up at her mom, a little surprised. "No, Mom, not at all. I was nervous at the beginning . . . sure, but Laurel Hill is great." She added, "God really found us a great place, didn't He?"

Mrs. Anderson smiled, and answered, "Yes, dear, He really has taken care of us. I'm glad you're happy here too." She leaned over and gave Maggie a big hug and a kiss and added, "You'd better get ready. We've got to be at Fun Land by eleven o'clock!"

When everyone was together in the parking lot of Fun Land, the girls were laughing and talking, excited to start the day. Mrs. Bloom had come along to help chaperone the girls with Mrs. Anderson, and she announced, "Okay, girls, now does everybody know what time and place we are meeting for lunch?"

Nikki answered for the group, "Yes, ma'am. We're meeting at the picnic tables near the batting cages at one o'clock for lunch."

"All right, then," replied Mrs. Anderson, "you girls enjoy yourselves. We'll see you later."

So, the girls took their tokens and made a mad dash into the park. Nikki and Maggie headed straight for the batting cages.

"I've wanted to do this since last season ended!" Maggie said as she selected a bat.

"I know, it's like practicing whenever you want to," Nikki replied, putting her helmet on and stepping into the cage beside Maggie.

After a couple of rounds of tokens, Nikki said, "You hit really good, Maggie."

"Thanks," she replied, "but I really need a new bat. Mine at home is too short, and I can barely make contact anymore!"

"Really?" Nikki answered with a knowing smile. "We'll have to see if we can find you a better one before next season." And with that, she added more tokens into the machine.

In the meantime, Jennifer and Katie had run over to the go-karts, prepared to do battle.

"I bet I can beat you around the track!" Katie said as she put on her helmet.

"No way!" Jennifer shouted as she climbed into her kart. "I remember how you drove the *bumper cars*. I'll beat you easy!"

The girls laughed as they moved their cars into position, and when the buzzer sounded, they were off! As they sped around the track, it was a close race. But in the end, Jennifer crossed the finish line a second before Katie.

"See, I told you!" Jennifer cheered as she stood up in her kart.

"Lucky break!" Katie laughed, as she took her goggles off. "Do you want to do it again?" And so the girls ran over to get back in line, and the race continued.

At the same time, Amy and Morgan had found their way over to the arcade.

"I love playing skeeball!" Amy shouted as she slid her tokens into the slot.

"I know," Morgan agreed. "It makes me feel like I'm at the boardwalk again. The first time I ever played this game was when we were at the beach."

After racking up a lot of tickets, and choosing their prizes, the girls moved over to the driving games.

"Okay, the first one to crash loses," Morgan announced.

"Deal!" Amy agreed as they put in their tokens and waited for the starting whistle.

When lunchtime rolled around, and everyone was settled at the picnic tables, Mrs. Anderson said the blessing on their meal, and everyone enjoyed a nice picnic lunch.

"Okay," Mrs. Anderson announced, "we have fried chicken, potato salad, coleslaw, and baked beans. Everyone help themselves, there's plenty." There were also potato chips, pretzels, dip, and pickles.

Everyone ate and enjoyed the delicious food, but they all made sure they left room for the cake.

When the birthday cake was brought out, Maggie shouted, "My favorite, red velvet cake! And look at the little hearts all over it! Thank you, Mom!" She gave her a big hug as everyone began to sing "Happy Birthday."

Finally, it was time for the gifts. Maggie began by opening Jennifer's present first. As she removed the paper and opened the box, she found a copy of *Huckleberry Finn*. "Oh, thank you, Jennifer, I love this book!" Maggie said as she hugged her.

"I know, I asked your mom what your favorite book was," replied Jennifer.

Next, Maggie opened Nikki's present, which was a new softball bat. "I can't believe it!" she exclaimed.

Nikki laughed and answered, "I told you we'd find you one! Now we can break it in together for next season."

Maggie picked up Amy's gift next. It was a framed print of one of Monet's paintings. "Oh, Amy, thank you. I love Monet's paintings!"

"I thought so. When I was in your room, I saw you had some, but I didn't think you had this one," Amy responded as Maggie hugged her.

Then, Maggie opened Morgan and Katie's gift. "We hope you like it!" Katie said as Maggie pulled off the wrapping paper.

"How did you do this?" Maggie asked in amazement as she sat staring at the framed picture of all the girls in front of the fountain at Adventure Park. The picture had been matted and everyone had signed it on the bottom.

"We had it blown up from our key chain picture," Morgan replied. "We thought it was a really good picture of all of us, and we wanted to show you how glad we are that you're here."

"Thank you so much," Maggie said as she gave them both a hug.

"Just two more gifts, Maggie," Mrs. Anderson announced as she pulled out two large boxes. "Your dad sent his a few days ago, but I had it hidden."

Maggie opened the box from her dad and found a new easel along with a black case. "Wow, a travel case for painting!" she shouted. "And a desktop easel! This'll be great. The other one is a little too tall sometimes," she added.

Finally, Maggie opened her Mother's gift. "Oh, Mom. I can't believe you got this for me!" she exclaimed as she revealed a set of oil paints in a wooden display case.

"Well, I know you've wanted to try oils for a while now. I have the paint thinner and other things at home to go along with it," Mrs.

Anderson replied. Maggie hugged her mom as everyone yelled "Happy Birthday, Maggie!"

After everything was cleaned up from lunch, and all the gifts were taken out to the car, everyone went and played a round of miniature golf.

"I've never seen a miniature golf course that had a giant gorilla on it!" Maggie laughed as she went to putt on the fourth hole.

"Sure," Jennifer replied, "just don't knock over his bananas!"

The girls, Mrs. Anderson, and Mrs. Bloom had a rousing match with Nikki finishing first and Katie coming in at a close second. When the game was finished, and everyone was ready to head home, Maggie thanked everyone one last time and hugged each girl. "Thank you so much. Today has been so much fun! I'm so glad that we moved to Laurel Hill."

"So are we," replied Amy, and everyone agreed as they each headed home for the evening.

That night, as Maggie sat at her desk in her room, she looked at all the gifts she had received for her birthday.

"What are you up to?" Mrs. Anderson asked from the doorway as Maggie looked up.

"I'm just writing my thank you cards so I don't forget to do it later," she responded with a smile.

Mrs. Anderson came into the room and sat on the bed. "Did you have a nice birthday?" she asked.

"Yeah, Mom, I really did. It was a lot of fun. Thank you so much!" Maggie replied.

"You're welcome, sweetie," Mrs. Anderson answered as she kissed Maggie on the head. "I'm glad you enjoyed it."

Later that night, as Maggie lay in bed, she prayed, "Lord, thank You for all that You have done. You've given me and Mom so much. You've brought me great friends, and You showed us a good church we can go to. Thank you for taking such good care of us. This move wasn't easy, especially for Mom. I know she misses Dad as much as I do. Please help us both not to be mad at him, and please help him to become saved. But most of all, help me to always remember to trust You, no matter what happens."

And as Maggie drifted off to sleep, she thought about all that had happened over those past few months, and she couldn't wait to see what the summer would bring next.

The End

About the Author

Erin Mackey currently lives in Martinsburg, West Virgina, with her husband, Larry. Erin worked as a nurse for more than thirteen years, including in pediatric nursing and has obtained a B.S. in Forensics, which is also a passion of hers. She enjoys spending her free time with her family, including her nieces and nephew: Emily age 13, Kate age 11, Morgan age 9, and Gabe age 7, who she says are her inspiration for writing children's books. She is currently working on the second book in the Laurel Hill Series.